Applesauce Day

by Lisa Amstutz

pictures by Talitha Shipman

Albert Whitman & Company
Chicago, Illinois

I spy the big pot on the counter right away.
  "Hooray!" I say. "It's Applesauce Day!"
  Hannah cheers.
  Ezra bangs his spoon.

After breakfast we load up the car
and drive to the apple orchard
just outside the city.

The air smells like ripe apples here.
I listen to the quiet.
There are no sirens or screeching tires,
only the buzzing of bees
and leaves rustling in the wind.

Then Hannah calls my name.

Jonathan

She's on her tippy-toes,
tugging at an apple.

I show her the trick Dad taught me last year:
twist and pull.
The apple pops right off.
Dad winks at me,
and we get to work.

Mom and Dad pick the high apples.
Hannah and I pick the low ones.
Ezra helps too.

Soon the baskets are full of rosy apples
ready to be smooshed into sweet, tangy applesauce.
We pack them up and head for Grandma's
big, roomy kitchen.

Grandma's waiting at the door.
Her smile matches mine as she hugs me tight.
"Ready to make applesauce?" she asks.

We lug the apple baskets
into the kitchen
and take our places.

This year, Ezra gets to help too.

Dad washes the apples,
and Grandma cuts them into quarters,
so they'll cook quickly.

Snick,

snick,

snick.

Ezra drops the apple quarters into the big steel pot.
Thunk, thunk, thunk.
It's heavy and wide and holds lots of apples—
the perfect pot for applesauce, Grandma says.
It looks like a regular pot to me.

FARM STAND

FRESH APPLES
GRANNY SMITH . . . 3
JONATHAN 2
McINTOSH 3

As we work, Mom tells us how she helped Grandma carry bushels of apples home from the market in their quiet Ohio town,

and how they cooked them in this very pot
when she was a little girl.

Grandma tells us how she helped *her* mother
pick apples from the old apple tree behind their house
on the windy Iowa prairie,

and how they too cooked them in this pot when she was a little girl.

I look at the pot again.
I wonder how many apples it has cooked
and what kind of stories it could tell...
if pots could talk.

Soon the warm scent of cooking
apples fills the air.
Their skins fade to pink as the
apples melt into mush.
Every now and then an air
bubble rises to the surface.

Mom scoops the hot apple mush into the food mill.
Hannah and I take turns cranking the handle
and pressing the apples into the funnel at the top.

Crank! Squish!
Crankity! Squish!

Applesauce squishes through the strainer
and flows like a river
into the pan waiting below.
Peels and seeds drop out
the end into a bowl.

I dip my finger into the applesauce for a taste.
It's so sweet it doesn't really need any sugar,
but we add a little anyway.
Then we scoop the applesauce into containers.

By now, our stomachs are rumbling.
Grandma sets out a plate of sandwiches
and a big bowl of warm applesauce.
She sprinkles cinnamon on top.
Mmmm…

We all take heaping helpings
and then seconds.
Ezra licks the bowl.

Then we go back to work.
Cutting…

and cooking…

and cranking...
Crank! Squish!
Crankity! Squish!

...until the baskets are empty
and the containers are full.
We fill Grandma's big freezer
and pack the rest in our car.

Finally, we say our good-byes
and head for home,
tired and sticky,
but full of stories
and smiles
and applesauce.

The car grows quiet.
I run my finger over the scratches
in the old metal pot.

Someday, I think,
when I grow up,
I will cook apples
in this very special pot
on Applesauce Day.

Applesauce Recipe

Ingredients

1–3 bushels of Apples (Cortland, Jonathan, McIntosh, Winesap, Transparent, Gala, Golden Delicious, and Fuji are good varieties for making applesauce.)

Sugar (to taste)

Cinnamon (optional)

1. With an adult's help, wash and quarter the apples, removing the calyx (the remains of the blossom at the bottom of the apple) and any bad spots. You do not need to remove the peel or core.

2. In a Dutch oven or stockpot on the stove, add about 1 inch of water to the apples, cover, and simmer. Stir occasionally and add more water as needed to keep them from sticking.

3. When the apples are mushy, run them through a food mill. This will remove the peels and seeds and spit out applesauce. Be careful—the apples are hot! Let an adult handle the pan.

4. Add a little sugar to sweeten the applesauce if desired. Then let it cool.

5. Put the applesauce into containers. Freeze it if desired for up to a year. Leave about an inch of space at the top of the container so the applesauce has room to expand as it freezes.

6. Repeat steps 1–5 until all the apples have been processed.

7. Serve your applesauce fresh or thaw if frozen. Add a dash of cinnamon if you'd like.

Note:

If you don't have a food mill, peel and core the apples before cooking them. After they are cooked, mash or puree them with a potato masher or blender. You can make the applesauce as chunky or as smooth as you like.

Yield:

1 bushel=approximately 12–15 quarts

Amazing Apple Facts

- Apples come in many different shades of red, yellow, and green.

- More than half of all commercially grown apples are eaten fresh. The rest are made into apple pie, applesauce, apple butter, apple juice, apple cider vinegar, apple cider, and more!

- Apples are harvested from late summer to fall.

- Apples belong to the rose family. The flowers on an apple tree look like wild roses.

- "An apple a day…" is good advice—apples are packed with fiber and contain vitamin C and other nutrients.

- The apple peel contains two-thirds of the fruit's fiber and lots of healthy antioxidants.

- Apples can be as small as golf balls or as large as softballs.

- A bushel of apples, approximately 42–48 pounds, makes 15–18 quarts of applesauce.

- Apple trees are pollinated by bees.

- Astronaut John Glenn, the first American to orbit the earth, took applesauce into space in squeezable aluminum tubes.

- Apple trees came to North America with early colonists from Europe. They dried some of the apples and used the rest to make apple cider, apple cider vinegar, and apple butter.

- In the early 1800s, John Chapman carried apple seeds westward to settlers in Pennsylvania, Ohio, Indiana, and Illinois. He became known as Johnny Appleseed.

To my wonderful, applesauce-loving family—LJA

To my Michael, who believes in me—TS

Library of Congress Cataloging-in-Publication
data is on file with the publisher.

Text copyright © 2017 by Lisa J. Amstutz
Pictures copyright © 2017 by Albert Whitman & Company
Pictures by Talitha Shipman
Published in 2017 by Albert Whitman & Company
ISBN 978-0-8075-0392-8
Printed in China
10 9 8 7 6 5 4 3 2 1 HH 22 21 20 19 18 17
Design by Jordan Kost

For more information about Albert Whitman & Company,
visit our website at www.albertwhitman.com.